THE ADVENTURE FRIENDS

Bright Star

Read more books in
THE ADVENTURE FRIENDS series!

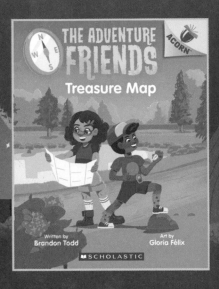

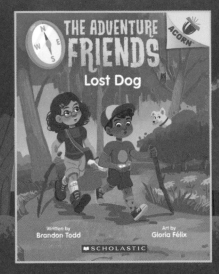

THE ADVENTURE FRIENDS

Bright Star

WRITTEN BY
Brandon Todd

ART BY
Gloria Félix

ACORN™
SCHOLASTIC INC.

For all my North Kansas City neighbors.
—BT

For my niece Spica, can't wait
to have adventures with you too.
—GF

Text copyright © 2023 by Brandon Todd
Illustrations copyright © 2023 by Gloria Félix

Library of Congress Cataloging-in-Publication Data

Names: Todd, Brandon, author. | Félix, Gloria, illustrator.
Title: Bright star / written by Brandon Todd ; illustrated by Gloria Félix.
Description: New York : Scholastic, Inc., [2023] | Series: The adventure friends ; 3 |
Audience: Ages 5–7. | Audience: Grades K–2 | Summary:
After visiting the library to search for new adventure ideas, Miguel
and Clarke go on a trip that is out of this world.
Identifiers: LCCN 2022036918 (print) | ISBN 9781338805888 (paperback) |
ISBN 9781338805895 (library binding)
Subjects: CYAC: Libraries—Fiction. | Imagination—Fiction. | Interstellar
travel—Fiction. | Maps—Fiction. | Friendship—Fiction. | LCGFT: Picture books.
Classification: LCC PZ7.1.T6125 Br 2023 (print) | DDC [E]—dc23
LC record available at https://lccn.loc.gov/2022036918

10 9 8 7 6 5 4 3 2 1   23 24 25 26 27

Printed in China   62
First printing, October 2023
Edited by Katie Carella
Book design by Brian LaRossa

TABLE OF CONTENTS

MEET THE CHARACTERS

adventure bag

walkie-talkie

compass

adventure socks

adventure fuel
(This is what Clarke calls her mom's trail mix!)

Clarke
New to town.
Loves planning,
drawing, and
ADVENTURE!

Miguel
Knows everyone in
town. Loves bugs,
surprises, and
ADVENTURE!

Spider
The mayor's
dog. Loves balls,
treats, and
ADVENTURE!

THE LIBRARY

Clarke and Miguel are friends.
They love going on adventures.
They are **adventure friends**.

Clarke looked at her **adventure map**.
She needed an idea for a new adventure.

Clarke called Miguel on her walkie-talkie. "Meet me at the library," she said.

"I'm on my way!" said Miguel.

Clarke was ready for adventure.

She grabbed the
adventure map.

She put on her
adventure socks.

And she headed out.

Miguel took out his compass.

He lined up the red needle with the **N**.
That's how to find **NORTH**, **SOUTH**,
EAST, or **WEST** on a compass.

Miguel walked **NORTH** to the library.

Miguel met Clarke on the library steps.
"Hey, Clarke! Why are we here?"
he asked.

"We need an idea for a new adventure,"
said Clarke. "So we are here
for **adventure books**."

"We'll find those here!" said Miguel.
"Let's go!"

It was Clarke's first time inside this library. It had more books than she had ever seen.

8

"Let's ask Lynda, the librarian, for help,"
said Miguel. "Her superpower is
finding books."

Miguel walked up to the desk.
"Hi, Lynda," he said. "Do you have
adventure books?"

Lynda smiled. "Hi, Miguel! Yes. Lots."

"We don't want to run out of adventures,"
said Clarke. "Can we see them all?"

"Okay!" said Lynda.

Lynda found books all over the library.
She handed them to Clarke one at a time.

Clarke passed them to Miguel.

Miguel added them to a library cart.

They found so many books!

Clarke and Miguel checked out
seven books.

Clarke put four books in her **adventure bag**.
Miguel carried the rest.

"Now we'll never run out of adventures,"
said Clarke.

THE SURPRISE

Clarke and Miguel sat in
their top secret fort.

Spider the dog was there.
He is an **adventure friend** too.

Spider was playing with a ball.

"I have an idea for our next adventure!"
said Miguel.

"Great!" said Clarke. "What is your idea?"

"I want it to be a surprise," said Miguel.
"Let's head home so I can get it ready."

Miguel, Clarke, and Spider walked home.

Then Miguel waved goodbye.
"I'll call you when the surprise is ready,"
he said.

Clarke stood in her yard.
Spider sat next to her.

"Now we wait," Clarke told Spider.

Spider brought Clarke his ball.
Clarke played catch with Spider.

Then Clarke read more **adventure books**.
The one about spies gave her an idea.

"Spider, you and I can be spies!"
Clarke told Spider.
"I'll show you what to do!"

Clarke showed Spider how to be quiet.
Spider barked at a squirrel.

Clarke showed Spider how to hide.
Spider pooped in the yard.

Clarke is very good at spying.
Spider is not.

Clarke snuck over to Miguel's house.

She saw Miguel in his backyard.

He was carrying two poles.

He also had piles of cardboard and flashlights.

Clarke thought about the surprise
adventure. She had a lot of ideas.

But none of her ideas seemed quite right.

Clarke was tired of being a spy.
So she went home.

Finally, Clarke's walkie-talkie buzzed.
"The surprise is ready!" Miguel said.

"YAY!" Clarke shouted.

She ran to Miguel's backyard.
Spider followed.

Miguel had a big smile.
"Our next adventure will take us
far away," he said.

"I can't wait to see this surprise!"
said Clarke.

He had built a spaceship.

Clarke was very surprised!

Clarke and Miguel were ready
for adventure.

"I've never been to space," Clarke said.

Miguel opened his space book.
"Space is very dark," he said.
"Stars are all around."

Clarke and Miguel looked at the sky.
It was bright and golden.

"Space is far, far away," said Miguel.
"It will be dark and starry when
we get there."

"Let's make a checklist for our trip," said Clarke.

"Good idea," said Miguel.

"**Adventure fuel**? Check!" Clarke said. "Space book? Check!"

Spider barked.

"Don't forget Spider!" Miguel said.

"We also need space helmets," said Miguel.

"Good idea," said Clarke.

"These will keep us safe outside," said Miguel.

Even Spider got a helmet.

"We are ready for blastoff," said Miguel.

Clarke, Miguel, and Spider entered the spaceship.

Then they began their long trip to space.

"How long will it take to get to space?" asked Clarke.

"Space is far, far away," said Miguel, "so it will take an hour."

Miguel set a timer.

"I'll eat a snack while we wait,"
said Clarke.

Clarke ate some **adventure fuel**.

Miguel read the space book.

"People go to space for lots of reasons,"
said Miguel. "Some want to find planets.
Some search for aliens."

"Why are we going to space?"
asked Clarke.

"For adventure!" replied Miguel.

Clarke hoped to find a new rock.

Miguel hoped to find a new friend.

Spider hoped to find a new ball.

The timer went off. "BEEP! BEEP! BEEP!"

Miguel, Clarke, and Spider put on
their helmets. They stepped out
of the spaceship.

The sky was dark. Stars were all around.

"Wow!" said Clarke.

"Welcome to space," said Miguel.

NORTH STAR

The **adventure friends** were in outer space. This was their first space adventure.

"Are we on a new planet?" asked Clarke.

"Maybe!" said Miguel.

"We should take notes about what we find," said Clarke.

She grabbed her colored pencils.

Miguel jumped on a trampoline.
"This planet is very floaty," he said.

Miguel grabbed a jar.
It had four holes in the lid.

Then he caught some aliens.
They glowed!

"Exploring space is hard work,"
said Miguel.

"It has been a long day," said Clarke.

They pulled out their sleeping bags.
They lay down and looked up at the sky.

The sky was filled with stars.

"Look at that bright star," said Clarke.

"Wow!" said Miguel. "It must be
the North Star."

"Can the North Star help you find which way is **NORTH**?" asked Clarke.

"Yep! It can be used like a compass," said Miguel. "A long time ago, the North Star helped explorers cross the ocean at night."

"Sometimes you can find pictures in the stars," said Miguel. "They tell stories!"

"Wow!" said Clarke. "I wonder if all the stars have a story. Let's make a map of the sky!"

She picked up a colored pencil.
She drew the stars in the sky.

Miguel connected the dots.

"Now our story is in the stars too,"
said Clarke.

Clarke and Miguel entered
the spaceship.

"Are you ready to go home?"
Miguel asked.

Clarke yawned. "Yes," she said. "This was
a great adventure."

The **adventure friends** began their long
trip home.

ABOUT THE CREATORS

Brandon Todd lives in North Kansas City, Missouri. When he was a kid, he made treasure maps of the woods by his house. The biggest treasure he found was three golf balls! He is the author and illustrator of a picture book called TOU-CAN'T!: A LITTLE SISTER STORY. The Adventure Friends is his first early reader series.

Gloria Félix was born and raised in Uruapan, a city in Michoacán, Mexico. This beautiful, small city is one of her biggest inspirations when it comes to her art. In addition to children's books, Gloria makes art for the animation industry. Her hobbies include walking, life drawing, and plein-air painting with her friends. Currently, she lives and paints in Guadalajara.

YOU CAN DRAW SPIDER!

1 Sketch a circle for Spider's head. Draw the outline of Spider's head and ears. (Sketch lightly so you can erase as you go!)

2 Draw his neck. Then sketch two circles for his body. Make the circle on the right smaller than the one on the left.

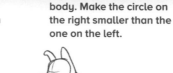

3 Add Spider's legs and feet. (Erase the sketch lines from the previous steps.)

4 Draw his wagging tail. Add his eyes, eyebrows, mouth, and nose too.

5 Add details to his ears and paws. Draw fur on his face and give him a tongue. Don't forget his collar!

6 Color in your drawing!

WHAT'S YOUR STORY?

Clarke, Miguel, and Spider go on a space adventure.
Imagine **you** go on a space adventure with them.
What does your spaceship look like?
What new things do you find in space?
Write and draw your story!